pish, posh,
said
Hieronymus Bosch

BY Nancy Willard

ILLUSTRATIONS BY THE DILLONS

HARCOURT BRACE JOVANOVICH, PUBLISHERS

SAN DIEGO   NEW YORK   LONDON

Requests for permission to make copies of
any part of the work should be mailed to:
Permissions Department,
Harcourt Brace Jovanovich, Publishers,
8th Floor, Orlando, Florida 32887.

Library of Congress Cataloging-in-Publication Data
Willard, Nancy.
Pish posh, said Hieronymus Bosch/by Nancy Willard;
illustrated by Leo, Diane, and Lee Dillon.
p.   cm.
Summary: An imaginative poem about
the fifteenth-century painter filled with medieval beasts
and other images from Bosch's world.
ISBN 0-15-262210-1
1. Bosch, Hieronymus, d. 1516 — Juvenile poetry.
2. Children's poetry, American.
[1. Bosch, Hieronymus, d. 1516 — Poetry. 2. American poetry.]
I. Dillon, Leo, ill. II. Dillon, Diane, ill. III. Title.
PS3573.I444P56   1991
811'.54 — dc19   86-3173

Printed in the United States of America
First edition
A B C D E

The illustrations in this book were underpainted in
acrylics on acetate and overpainted with oils.
The frame was sculpted and cast in silver, bronze, and
brass, then assembled on a wood frame by Lee Dillon.
The frame was photographed by Melitte Buchman.
Jacket frame dies by Wheeler Engraving, Santee, California
The illustrations were spot-varnished and printed
on 100-pound Natural Karma paper.
The display type and text type were hand-lettered
by the illustrators.
Color separations were made by Bright Arts, Ltd., Singapore.
Printed by Holyoke Lithograph, Springfield, Massachusetts
Bound by Book Press, Brattleboro, Vermont
Production supervision by Warren Wallerstein
Art direction by Michael Farmer
Designed by Leo and Diane Dillon

For James and Julie
— N. W.

To wives and housekeepers and mothers everywhere
— D. & L. & L. D.

Once upon a time there was an artist
named Hieronymus Bosch who loved odd creatures.
Not a day passed that the good woman who looked
after his house didn't find a new creature
lurking in a corner or sleeping in a cupboard.
To her fell the job of
    feeding them,
    weeding them,
    walking them,
    stalking them,
    calming them,
    combing them,
    scrubbing and tucking in all of them —
until one day...

"I'm quitting your service, I've had quite enough
of your three-legged thistles asleep in my wash,
of scrubbing the millstone you use for a dish,
and riding to shops on a pickle-winged fish."

"Pish, posh,"
said Hieronymus Bosch.

"How can I cook for you? How can I bake
when the oven keeps turning itself to a rake,
and a beehive in boots and a pear-headed priest
call monkeys to order and lizards to feast?

"The nuns were quiet. I'd rather be bored
and hang out their laundry in sight of the Lord,

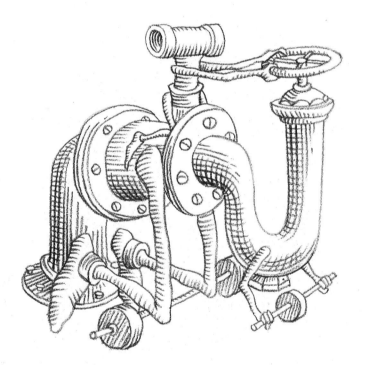

"than wrestle with dragons to get to my sink
while the cats chase the cucumbers, slickity-slink."

"They go slippity-slosh,"
said Hieronymus Bosch.

"I don't mind the ferret, I do like the bee.
All witches' familiars are friendly to me.
I'd share my last crust with a pigeon-toed rat,
and some of my closest relations are cats."

"My aunt was a squash,"
said Hieronymus Bosch.

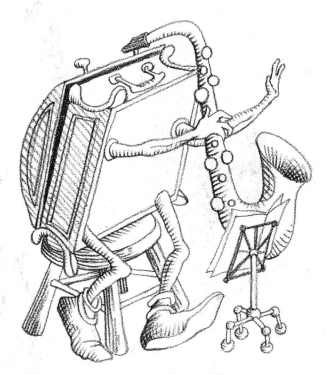

She packed her fur tippet, her second-best hat.

(The first was devoured by a two-headed bat.)

WITH a pain in HER BACK AND a FOG in HER HEAD,

SHE WALKED TWENTY-TWO MILES AND COLLAPSED INTO BED.

THAT NIGHT SHE AWOKE TO a TERRIBLE ROAR.

Her suitcase YAWNED AND UNLEASHED ON THE FLOOR

a MOLE in a HABIT,

    a THISTLEDOWN RABBIT,

      a TROOP OF JACKDAWS,

        a THREE-LEGGED DISH,

THE PICKLE-WINGED FISH, AND a HEAD WEARING CLAWS.

"Take us under your wing, take us up on your back,"
they howled, while the claws murmured, "clickety-clack."

"They're not what I wished for. When women are young
they want curly-haired daughters and raven-haired sons.
In this vale of tears we must take what we're sent,
feathery, leathery, lovely, or bent."

WITH HER suitcase and TIPPET secure on THE DISH,
SHE CLAMBERED ABOARD THE PICKLE-WINGED FISH.

Hieronymus rose from a harrowing night,

saw salvation approaching, and crowed with delight.

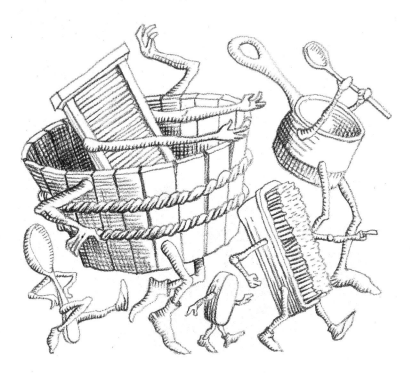

"My lovey, my dear, have you come back to stay?
Let the crickets rejoice and the mantises pray,
let the lizards do laundry, the cucumbers cook.
I shall set down new rules in my gingerbread book.

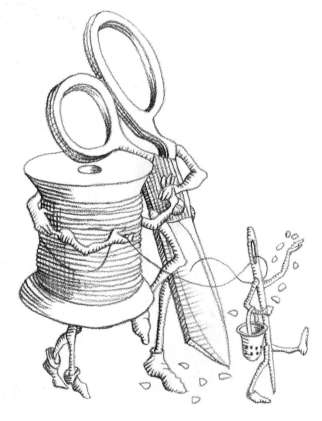

"The dragon shall wear a gold ring in his nose
and the daws stoke the fire and the larks mend our clothes
forever and ever, my nibble, my nosh,
till death do us part," said Hieronymus Bosch.

ABOUT HIERONYMUS BOSCH

Artist Hieronymus Bosch was born in the 1450s in Hertogenbosch, Netherlands. He is especially known for the bizarre creations that populate his work — people and everyday objects twisted into fantastic shapes and behaving in impossible ways. Although, in this book, Bosch's creatures served primarily as a departure point and a source of inspiration, it is interesting to note that Bosch's paintings have been a source of curiosity among art historians, researchers, and the public for hundreds of years. And although many books have been written about the work, the meaning behind the puzzles, fables, and unusual images in his art remains mysterious. He died in 1516.

ABOUT THE AUTHOR

Nancy Willard's fascination with the odd creatures found in Bosch's sketches and paintings goes back to when she was working on her master's thesis in medieval studies at Stanford. Since childhood she has shared her home with an assortment of cats and other pets and was led to wonder what life would be like in a household filled with even more peculiar creatures — like those invented by Bosch. The result is the highly imaginative poem in this book. Nancy Willard is the author of more than twenty books for children and adults, and she has won many honors for her work, including the John Newbery Medal for *A Visit to William Blake's Inn*. She teaches at Vassar College and at the Breadloaf Writers' Conference, and she lives with her husband, Eric Lindbloom, in Poughkeepsie, New York. They have one son, James.

ABOUT THE ILLUSTRATORS

It was a stroke of good fortune to find illustrators who not only knew Bosch's work intimately but had been strongly influenced by him. The evidence of this can be found in Leo and Diane Dillon's fantasy and science-fiction artwork on book jackets and album covers. The Dillons met more than thirty years ago in art school and have worked together ever since. Among their numerous awards, they have won the Caldecott Medal twice, and their recent paintings in *Aïda* received the Coretta Scott King Award for Illustration. In 1991, they received honorary doctorates of fine arts from the Parsons School of Design. Lee Dillon, their son, is a sculptor and painter. He handcrafted the frame for the *Pish, Posh, Said Hieronymus Bosch* illustrations out of silver, bronze, and brass. His work on the illustrations marks his first collaboration on paintings with his parents. The Dillons live in Brooklyn, New York.